Saturdays Are for Stella

Candy Wellins

illustrated by Charlie Eve Ryan

PAGE
STREET
KiDS

George loved Saturdays.

Saturdays were for Stella.

Sometimes George and Stella
went out on Saturdays . . .

to the park,
to the dinosaur museum,

and sometimes even as far as downtown.

Normally George did not like going downtown.
Downtown trips without Stella meant

waiting in boring offices,

eating strange foods,

and trying on scratchy clothes.

But with Stella, George ate frozen yogurt, threw pennies in fountains, and rode on carousels.

Whenever they passed a toy store—and they *always* passed a toy store—George went home with something fun.

Sometimes George and Stella stayed in on Saturdays . . .

hosting ninja tournaments,

fighting off alien attacks,

and sometimes doing really unusual things too.

Stella knew how to make cinnamon rolls
without popping open a tube.
She owned giant, flat Frisbees and
could get them to play music.

And she never, ever tired of reading
George's favorite books, listening
to his favorite jokes, or admiring his
growing collection of bouncy balls.

**George kept a running list
of the best things about Stella:**

1. The way her arms wrap me in the biggest,
   best hugs when I need them most

2. The way she loves doing everything with me . . .

3. And also doing nothing at all

One Saturday George woke up late.
He dressed himself and packed a bag with
everything he might need for a day with Stella.

When he walked downstairs, he found
his parents still in their pajamas.

Dad's eyes were red, and Mom's nose was
all stuffy. George kept his distance.
He didn't want to catch a cold on a Saturday.

Saturdays were for Stella.

But then Dad explained that it wasn't a cold that made his eyes red.

And Mom explained why George couldn't see Stella today or any other Saturday.

From then on, George hated Saturdays.

He tried to focus on remembering Stella,
but it was hard. His parents tried to help.

But carousel rides
made him queasy.

Cinnamon rolls
tasted sad.

And even his favorite
jokes made him cry.

So, George used a big black pen to cross out
all the Saturdays on his calendar.

His parents started marking their calendar too,
and soon there were more trips downtown than ever before.

George didn't have to eat funny foods or try on scratchy clothes,
but there was plenty of waiting in boring offices.

And though they often stopped at the toy store
on the way home, George never went home with anything fun.

Just when George thought he
couldn't take another Saturday . . .

Stella arrived.

She wasn't exactly like his Stella,
but there was something strangely familiar about her.

Now George doesn't have time to be sad on Saturdays.

He's too busy going out with Stella to the park, to the dinosaur museum, and sometimes even as far as downtown.

George has introduced her to the wonders of frozen yogurt, fountains, and carousel rides.

Sometimes George and Stella stay in on Saturdays.

They still have ninja tournaments and fight off alien invasions,
but sometimes they throw dance parties and tea parties too.
George always makes a batch of cinnamon rolls to share.

One Saturday George makes a list
of his favorite things about Stella:

1. The way her arms wrap me in the biggest,
best hugs when I need them most

2. The way she loves doing everything with me . . .

3. And also doing nothing at all

George loves Saturdays.

Saturdays are for Stella.

In memory of Mickey Larson and Liz Fennel,
two stellar grandmas.
—C. W.

Dedicated to Nana and Pop-Pop
for all the joy they bring.
—C. E. R.